When My

Fell Through the Moon

Samuel Risso Rossetti

RECOVERY
INC.

For resources and more information visit
www.recoveryinc.org

Dedicated to my godson Sil and anyone who has
been affected by this disease.

Just remember:
Every day is not going to be a good day, but
there's something good in every day.

The sights and sounds of fall were in the air as golden, crisp leaves danced in the wind. Taylor, a bright young student was in awe of the leaves falling from the trees as she stared out her class window.

Right before the 2 PM bell sounded, she learned about the musical tryouts for the school's fall musical in her choir class. She had dreamed about being in the musical since she was in second grade.

She was now in fourth grade and confident that she might have a chance. Taylor attended a summer choir camp and was ready for the challenge.

As she rode the bus home that afternoon, Taylor could not wait to share the news of the musical tryouts with her parents. When the bus dropped her off at her house, she skipped to the front door with complete happiness about the tryout opportunity.

Her mom said, "Taylor, what a smile! What's going on with you?" Taylor said, "Mom, you won't believe it. There are going to be tryouts next week for the annual fall musical. I think I have a chance this year! All the practice from choir camp really boosted my confidence to try out this year."

Her mom replied, "I am so excited for you. Let me know how I can help?" Taylor replied, "The school needs parent volunteers for our rehearsal days. Do you think you and Dad can help? Oh, and where's dad? I want to tell him too." Her mom replied, "He is busy in his office right now. We can share the news with him later."

As dinner time arrived, the family sat down for a yummy steak dinner. Taylor was excited to share the news with her dad. She said, "Dad, I am going to try out for the school musical next week. They need parent volunteers to help. Do you think you can come?" Her dad was in a good mood today. He replied, "Of course Taylor, I would love to help you. I'll be there."

Taylor was very excited that her parents were willing to help. After dinner, she started practicing her lines with her stuffed animals in her room. Her mom loved singing and coached Taylor with her audition song too. The family dog, Buddy even helped Taylor. He sat on her bed and listened to her throughout the evening.

As the days passed, Taylor practiced morning, noon and night. Soon, her big tryout day had arrived. The family's antique clock chimed seven beautiful bells. Taylor shouted, "Dad, today is the audition day. I want to arrive early to school so I can practice with my friends. Can you drive me?"

Taylor's mom had to leave for work early today. As her dad opened a bright orange bottle, and chewed on a tiny white tablet, he replied, "I can't drive you today. You will have to ride the bus."

Taylor felt saddened that she would have to take the bus, but knew her dad had been looking sick and needed rest. She also wondered why he always had that orange plastic bottle with him. She grabbed her pink unicorn backpack and met the school bus with a bright smile.

As the golden sun rose in the sky, Taylor walked quickly to the school auditorium for the morning tryouts. The musical's theme was about Earth and the solar system. Taylor hoped to play the lead part of the moon. She wanted this part so bad because her dad always said he loved her to the moon and back.

As she took to the stage, she took a deep breath and began to sing. In the past, she was always nervous singing in front of people. This time she felt like a different person because of her choir camp experience. She sang with confidence and energy.

Her teacher, Ms. Johnson said, "Well done, Taylor. I think that you really improved from last year. Great job! I will post the results tomorrow morning in the cafeteria."

Later that evening, Taylor wrote in her glittery, blue diary about her audition and hopes of being in the play.

The next day arrived and Taylor enjoyed a delicious pancake breakfast with her mom. Her mom said, "Taylor, call me at lunch when you find out the results." Taylor replied, "I could not sleep last night because I was so nervous!" Taylor asked her mom why her dad was not eating with them that morning. Taylor's mom replied, "He is really sleepy, but will join us for dinner tonight."

The bus soon dropped Taylor off at school, and she scurried to the cafeteria to see if her teacher had posted anything. As Taylor reached the bulletin board, she saw a long line of students trying to find their names. She waited patiently in line for her turn.

She ran her finger down the poster slowly scanning for her name. Suddenly, she saw her name in bright red letters that read, "Taylor will play part of the moon." She was in complete awe and she almost dropped to the floor with excitement and shock that she got the part. Her friends cheered her name and gave her several high fives.

She called her mom during lunch at the school office to share the awesome news. Her mom congratulated her and told her they would celebrate by going to her favorite pizza place. When she arrived home, Buddy met her at the door. He gave her a big paw handshake. She ran to the living room to share the news with her dad. He was sound asleep on the couch.

Taylor's mom soon came into the living room and cheered, "Taylor, you are my princess moon! I am so very proud of you. When is the rehearsal? We want to be there for you." Her dad woke up and said, "What's all the noise? Taylor, did you make it?" She replied, "Yes, dad, I am going to play the part of the moon." Her dad replied, "Terrific, I can help design and paint the props for the play."

As Taylor laid her head on her pillow that night, she was so happy that she got the part. Most of all, she was glad that her parents would be a part of the play too.

The first rehearsal was later on that week. Taylor looked at the gigantic wood boards that would soon be the props. Her mom arrived and gave her a big warm hug. She said, "Taylor, what can I do?" Taylor said, "My teacher said that she is holding a parent meeting at 4 PM in the gym. Where's dad?" Her mother replied, "He just called me and said he was running late."

Taylor was puzzled and sad. She said, "But he said he would be here." Taylor's mom said, "He will be here soon." Taylor's friends brought over some oil paints to start decorating the backdrop of the sky.

As Taylor started to paint, she saw her dad walk through the backstage door. Taylor shouted, "Dad, I am over here." Her dad replied, "Taylor, sorry I am late." Taylor said, "There's a meeting for the parents in the gym. It started 30 minutes ago."

She saw the other students stare at her dad. This made her feel like she had done something wrong.

Taylor's dad slowly ventured to the gym.

A month passed and Taylor was becoming even more confident in her role playing the moon. She also landed the solo. Singing was one of her favorite things to do. She loved singing all types of songs. She even used her purple rhinestone hairbrush as a microphone to practice like she was on stage.

There was another parent meeting about making more stage props. Taylor had her heart set on her dad making the gigantic yellow glittery moon as he was an architect. During dinner, she said, "Dad, there is a really important meeting tomorrow about the props. I told my teacher that you could make us a cool moon!" He replied, "Taylor, I will be there. I will see about bringing some boards from my shop too."

Her mom said, "Taylor, I will be there too. I told my job that I needed to help you with the school play. They are very excited for you and want to come see you sing in the musical."

As the warm sun shined on the school steps, Taylor made her way to the auditorium to wait for her parents in the audience. She saw her mom waving at her from the door. She noticed that her dad was not with her mom. In that moment, she felt a tear rolling down her cheek. Taylor started to think that maybe her dad wasn't interested in her musical role anymore and maybe she had done something wrong once again.

As her mom reached the seats, she said, "Taylor, I brought some red velvet cupcakes for everyone. I selected your favorite ones with the vanilla icing in the middle." Her mom noticed she looked sad. She said, "Taylor, don't worry, your dad will be here soon."

As the principal and choir teacher started the parent meeting, Taylor watched the clock as her dad was still missing.

Later that evening when Taylor and her mom returned home, she saw her dad sitting at the kitchen table along with Buddy. Taylor said, "Dad, where were you? We were waiting for you! Remember, I told my teacher that you could design the moon?" He replied, "I am sorry, I didn't feel well this afternoon."

Taylor munched on her favorite chips and wrote in her diary. She wrote about her hurt feelings. Taylor also wrote about her dad not showing up for the school meeting. She began feeling that she was the problem.

As Taylor was about to fall asleep, her mom walked into her room. She said, "Taylor, I was so glad to meet the other parents today and be a part of your special day at rehearsal. When is the next one? I will make sure that your dad is there for the next meeting." Taylor said, "The next volunteer day is on Friday. Will you please encourage dad to be there this time?" Her mom replied, "I spoke with your dad. He told me he would cut out the moon tonight and bring it to school on Friday."

Friday arrived and the students, with all different size paint brushes in hand, were busy finishing the final touches for the musical props. They had decorated a sun, clouds, flowers, and mountains, and were almost done. They set up a large paper moon in the meantime, so they could see how the stage would look from the seats.

All they needed now was the special wooden moon prop that Taylor's dad was making. Taylor's teacher walked over to her and said, "Taylor, will your dad be here soon? We need the moon to set up the stage."

In that moment, Taylor's dad walked in with the gigantic wooden moon. His steps were slow and almost like he was swaying from side to side. With the big moon over his shoulder, he started walking up the stairs toward the stage.

Suddenly, he lost his balance, tripped, and began to tumble down. He was still in mid fall as he set the moon down on the stage and fell backwards over it.

He lay there on the stage right next to Taylor and her friends looking up at them. Taylor screamed, "Dad, are you ok?" Her dad replied, very slowly, "Yes, I just tripped on the paint brushes that were on the floor." Her mom rushed over and helped her dad to his feet.

Her teacher was relieved he did not hurt anyone and gathered the students together to take a break outside.

Taylor's mom helped her in the car and drove them home. As they made their way home, Taylor had tears falling down her face. She felt that her dad's fall was her fault. When they returned home, Taylor's mom told her that she wanted to talk with her after dinner. She said, "Taylor, after you walk Buddy, I will meet you in your room."

Taylor's mom walked toward her room and knocked on the door. Taylor with a quiet voice said, "Come on in, mom." Taylor was listening to her favorite song while she was cleaning up her room. Taylor's mom sat down beside her on her bed and said, "Taylor, I need to talk to you about your dad."

Taylor said, "Mom, I already know what you are going to say. I know it's my fault that dad has been acting funny. I know how he likes sports and maybe he is not interested in my musical."

Her mother replied in a quiet and calm voice, "Taylor, it is not your fault. You are a very special child. I want you to understand what is really going on with your dad."

Buddy entered Taylor's room and laid beside Taylor's fuzzy panda slippers.

Taylor looked at her mom with tears rolling down her cheeks and replied, "Today dad's fall really scared me. He doesn't act like himself anymore."

Her mom replied, "I want you to know that you are not alone and you don't need to be afraid. I am here for you. Something very serious is happening with your dad.

"Your father has a disease. It is called addiction. It means that your father has been taking drugs to feel good and without them he feels sick. This is the reason you see him carrying around a tiny orange bottle all the time. The drugs are bad for his health. They make him sick, but he feels bad without them. The drugs also make him act funny and hurt our feelings."

Taylor's mom continued to explain, "Addiction is a type of sickness that requires help to get better. It is like your grandmother's cancer. She needed help and treatment to feel better.

"Remember when she was in the hospital? Well now your dad needs to go to treatment. This time away will allow him to get better. He will need to be gone for about a month or more.

"Remember Buddy's hip problems and how he needed special treatment so he could start feeling better again?"

Taylor replied, "So, it is like that time when I had the stomach flu and I needed to go to the doctor?"

Her mom said, "Yes, it is an illness, but your dad's addiction disease may require a longer treatment. He will have to stay in treatment so he can get the help his disease requires."

Taylor whispered, "Can I catch the disease from him?"

Her mom replied, "No. You cannot get it from hanging out with your dad. A person has to take drugs and rely on them so they can feel good every day. This type of behavior leads to addiction."

Then Taylor said, "I understand, but what if someone finds out. What will my friends think about me?"

Her mom took Taylor's hand and said, "Taylor, you don't have to be afraid. Your dad still loves you and it's not your fault. You can always talk to me. I am your mom. I will always be here for you. Our home is a safe place to talk about your dad's illness.

"In regard to your friends and other classmates, I can tell you that there are other students in your school with families who share the same addiction problem. It's a secret in a lot of families. This is why I want you to know that you can always talk to me about it. There is also a school counselor, Ms. Renee, who you can share your feelings with about your dad. She will listen to you anytime you feel scared at school or want to talk to her while your dad is away. It is also not a secret in our home. If you want, I can introduce you to her next week."

Taylor squeezed her mom's hand and said, "Thank you, mom. I feel better already."

As Taylor gazed at the crescent moon rising through her window, she was becoming sleepier by the moment. She was less afraid of her dad's problem now. Taylor asked her mom one more question, "Should I leave him alone when he comes home from treatment?"

Her mom replied, "When he returns from his treatment, we need to be kind and thoughtful with him as it may take some more time for him to feel better. He might even need to go to some more classes and meetings to help him feel even healthier."

Taylor, with her big brown eyes, looked up at her mom and whispered, "So, it's really not my fault after all. You helped me understand that I was never a part of the problem. I wish I could help him, though."

Her mom replied, "Taylor, it was never your fault, and you need to keep being your bright shining and happy self while you are around him every day. That will help him feel better too."

Taylor then climbed into her bed, and said, "Thank you mom for helping me understand what is going on with dad now. I don't feel afraid anymore and know that I am not alone. If I am scared, I will come talk to you."

Taylor's mom gave her a warm hug and kissed her princess goodnight and left her room to go to sleep.

A month passed and Taylor was feeling much better about what was happening with her dad. She shared her feelings with her mom every night at dinner, and even wrote in her diary about what was happening with her dad.

The fall musical was on Saturday and she was super excited for this special day. Her mom spent the next few days helping Taylor with her costumes along with practicing her songs. Saturday soon arrived, and the fall musical was at 5 PM. Taylor grabbed her blue and pink dress and her pink sparkly shoes and said, "Mom, I am ready to go now." She gave Buddy a handshake for good luck and hurried to the car.

As Ms. Johnson, her choir teacher, called everyone to their places on stage, Taylor peaked through the brown velvet stage curtain. She could only see her mom in the audience. She still had hope though that her dad would arrive to see her perform.

The curtain soon opened, and Taylor stepped out into the spotlight. As she sang the last line of her song, she saw her dad walk down the aisle and take his seat next to her mom. Seeing her dad made her heart beam and sing even louder with joy. Thanks to her mom's guidance and support, she now understood that her dad would be there for her. But she knew, like with any sickness, that it would take some time for her dad to heal and feel like himself again.

Taylor ended her song on a high note and bowed after her song was over. Everyone stood up and shouted, "Bravo, Taylor!"

After the musical was over, her parents met her on stage and gave her a beautiful bouquet of pink roses. She reached out to her dad and gave him a big hug and said, "I love you, dad. You look like you are feeling a lot better. Mom and I are here for you!"

Her dad replied, "Taylor, thank you, I am feeling better and I am getting stronger each day." Then, the family gave each other a huge group hug.

They left the show walking hand in hand off into the starry night to enjoy Taylor's favorite ice cream at home with Buddy.

About the Author

Samuel "Risso" Rossetti has dedicated his life to helping addicts and their families deal with the devastating effects of addiction. He is a recovering addict himself, with multiple years sober, and understands the effects of addiction on the addict and on everyone that loves them. He founded Recovery Inc. to provide addicts and their families a resource for help.

After his godson came to visit him in Florida over Christmas break he became inspired to write a children's book for kids who have grown up around addiction. He saw an issue with the existing books out there for children that just told kids "don't do drugs". He wanted to explain to children, in a way that they would understand, what is happening with a parent or loved one who is addicted to drugs and that it is not their fault.

For resources and more information visit
www.recoveryinc.org

Printed in Great Britain
by Amazon